FIRST CHAPTER BOOKS

TIME
CHRONICLES

READ WITH
Biff,
Chip &
Kipper

The Power of the Cell

Written by David Hunt
and illustrated by Alex Brychta

Before reading

- Read the back cover text and page 4. What do you think the Cell actually is?
- Look at page 5. Why do you think the TimeWeb needs the Cell?

After reading

- What clues could the events in the story have given Michael Faraday about electricity?

Book quiz

1 Who was hiding the Cell?
 a Michael
 b Tyler
 c Kipper
2 Who was the woman?
3 What happened when the Cell landed in the box of copper?

See p45 for the book quiz answers!

The story so far ...

The Cell is a vital part of the TimeWeb, an ancient computer that can detect where Virans are attacking the past.

While Biff and Chip wait anxiously in the Time Vault, the other children face extreme danger.

Can they bring the Cell safely back to Mortlock, the Time Guardian? Or will the Virans get to it first?

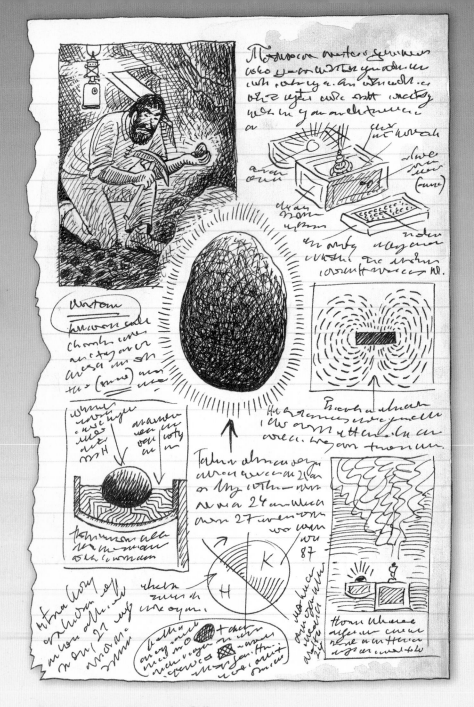

Part of the TimeWeb – the Cell

"... the Cell gives the TimeWeb its power."

Theodore Mortlock – Time Guardian

Chapter 1

Nadim and Wilma shot through the door of the Circularium. They spun back through time.

The doorway opened and Nadim was jolted to the ground. Wilma landed next to him.

For a moment it looked as if someone else was going to follow them.

But then the doorway vanished.

Nadim and Wilma were in a narrow unlit alley that went between tall buildings. They shivered in the freezing night air.

They did not notice the shadowy figures watching them from a dark doorway.

Wilma felt a deep chill. She wrapped her arms round her body. "We'd better find out where we are," she said.

The alley led to a cobbled street. Ahead was a warm glow of light. As they walked towards it, the figures looked at each other and nodded.

The light came from a bookbinder's shop, full of leather-covered books. In a frame on the door was a newspaper. It said:

The London Gazette. 13th October 1805.

Steam. Is it the power of the future?

"Steam!" chuckled Nadim. "Imagine if we had steam–powered computers!"

Suddenly a stone landed at Wilma's feet. It had been thrown from across the street.

Out of the darkness, a woman stepped forward. "Over here!" she hissed.

"Be ready to run," whispered Nadim, as they crossed back towards the alley.

"I saw you in the alley," the woman said. "I know why you are here."

Wilma's mind raced. What had the woman seen? What did she know? But Wilma wasn't expecting what the woman said next.

"Mortlock sent me to help you," continued the woman. "There isn't much time to explain."

Nadim's chest tightened. He thought back to the Time Vault. Had Mortlock mentioned others being sent?

The woman stepped closer. The air seemed
to freeze. "We can't stay here," she said,
crossing the road. "It is too dangerous."

"What do you mean?" stuttered Wilma as
they followed after her.

"The Virans are close. If *I* saw you, they
may have seen you too."

The woman pushed open the door of the bookbinder's shop. "In here, and quickly," she urged.

As they went in, the woman turned and looked back to the dark alley. She nodded before closing the door.

A figure moved from the shadows. He had understood her signal. Their plan was beginning to take shape.

Chapter 2

The first thing they noticed in the shop was the smell. The air was thick with the smell of leather, glue, varnish and smoke.

There were books everywhere. Towards the back of the shop stood a large desk covered in tools – needles, threads, rolls of cloth, mallets, knives, and bottles of ink. A single lamp glowed dimly in the gloom.

Nadim glanced nervously around.
Through a door at the back of the shop,
he could see what looked like a homemade
laboratory. Above a large fireplace were
shelves stacked with bottles and tubes,
cylinders, coils of wire and copper sheets.

"What is this place?" murmured Wilma.

"It's a safe place," breathed the woman,
"for now."

"Safe?" asked Wilma. "How do you know?
Who are you?"

The woman smiled. "Mortlock sent me
to help you find the Cell. It is a powerful
magnet called a lodestone. It is very
dangerous. It will react badly if it is put near
certain things."

"I see. Like electricity reacts badly with
water," nodded Nadim.

"So have you found the Cell?" asked Wilma.

"I am close to finding it," said the woman. "But so are the Virans." She paused. The lamplight flickered in the cold air.

She picked up a book. "A boy called Michael works here. I think he knows where the Cell is hidden. I have been watching him."

"So where is he?" asked Wilma.

"I lost sight of him this evening," said the woman. "We may be too late. The Virans may already have him ... and the Cell."

Suddenly, above their heads, they could hear the dull thud of footsteps. Someone was coming down the stairs.

Everyone froze. "Virans?" hissed Wilma.

"Quiet!" ordered the woman. "Be ready."

Chapter 3

A figure entered the back room and
began searching the laboratory. "Why
can't I find it?" the figure muttered. "Ah,
here it is!"

"The Cell?" whispered Nadim.

The figure lit a candle. It was a boy about
Wilma's age. He was holding a large jar.

The woman coughed gently. The boy
spun round in surprise and dropped the jar,
which smashed on the stone floor.

"I am sorry," he stuttered. "I thought I had closed the shop." He looked at the jar on the floor. "You see, I like to do experiments in my spare time. Anyway, can I help you?"

"There's not much time," said the woman. "Are you Michael? Michael Faraday?"

"Do you know the name Mortlock?" Wilma added.

Michael gulped. "Yes. I was asked to look after something for him, but ..."

"There is no time for this!" snapped the woman. "Where have you put the Cell? The Virans are close, and who knows what damage they could do with its power."

"I don't have it," Michael said, quietly. "My friend Tyler is hiding it for me," he added. "I will take you to him."

Suddenly the candles flickered and then died. Standing in the doorway was the shadowy figure from the alleyway. He thrust out a hand. "Give!" said the Viran.

"Run!" shouted Michael. "This way!"

Chapter 4

K ipper could remember going into the Circularium and spinning back in time, but where was he now? He was lying on a bundle of rags, but other than that, he wasn't sure.

A boy in a wheelchair was looking down at him. "I'm Tyler," the boy said. "Who are you?"

"Where am I?" murmured Kipper.

"There's a funny thing," said Tyler. "One minute I'm working away on my printing press, then the next, you're lying on that pile of rags. How did you just appear like that?"

"Er ... Mortlock sent me," said Kipper.

Tyler's face went pale. "Mortlock?" he gasped. "I know about all that TimeWeb stuff! My mate Faraday told me. Clever lad. Into science. He can work stuff out. He said if anyone mentioned Mortlock I had to tell him, and be quick-sharp about it."

Tyler wheeled himself across the room and pushed open a door. "I'll get my coat," he said. "Then we can go and find Faraday."

Beyond the door was another large room. In the centre of the room was a metal printing machine. On the floor were barrels of ink. Hanging from the ceiling was a heavy frame for drying paper.

"Do you live here?" asked Kipper.

"Live here, work here," said Tyler. "I'm an orphan. Lucky I could read so I got a job here. I make up the tray of words for each page we print. We even print illustrations, using sheets of copper. That's how I know Faraday. I print pages, he binds them together into books."

Suddenly, there was a noise from the
street. Tyler crossed to the door. In rushed
Michael, Wilma and Nadim.

"Nadim! Wilma!" shouted Kipper. "Am I
glad to see you."

"Ssssh!" panted Michael. "Virans! They'll
hear us. We've just been chased by one."

"Oh no!" said Wilma. "Where's the
woman? What if the Viran caught her?"

Wilma started for the door. "We must go back!" she cried. But to her relief, the woman appeared.

"I think we've lost him," the woman gasped. "But we must hurry." She looked at Michael. "We need the Cell, and quickly. Is it here?"

Michael looked at Tyler. Tyler nodded.

Tyler broke open a barrel. He dipped his
hand in and pulled up a heavy lump of
metal, dripping with ink.

"I hid it like you told me, Michael," he
said. "Nobody would think it was in here."

The woman gave a wheezing laugh.
"Clever!" she said.

At that moment the door crashed open.

"The Viran's found us!" shouted Nadim.

The Viran gave a menacing snarl.

"Give!" he rasped.

At the same time, both Wilma and the woman lunged towards Tyler. The woman grabbed the Cell.

The woman smiled. "It's mine!" she whispered. Wilma looked at her, puzzled. What she saw made her gasp. The woman's eyes became cold and pale. Her freezing claw-like hand grabbed Wilma's shoulder and she pushed her out of the way.

"Virans!" screamed Tyler. "She's one of them!"

Chapter 5

"So you are Mortlock's new hope?" the
woman laughed. "It's almost too easy."

She reached across to the printing press
and picked up a page. They watched,
horrified, as the words on the page
disappeared under a black stain that spread
from her fingers. "We can destroy history
as easily as I can destroy these words,"
she smirked.

The man started to laugh. "What fools you are! You will never save history. We will destroy history, and spread darkness. Without the Cell you are finished."

The woman turned. Tyler saw his chance. He kicked over the barrel of ink. The woman slipped on the thick, black puddle that poured out of it. As she fell, the Cell flew across the room.

The Cell landed in a box of copper printing sheets. Instantly the whole box fizzed with a massive charge of power.

The man scuttled toward the sparking box. Without thinking Nadim grabbed a rope tied to a hook. It was the rope that held up the large drying frame above them. It fell with a crash, knocking the man to the floor. "What fools *you* are!" shouted Nadim.

For a second, all was still. All was silent, except the crackling of strange coloured sparks as the Cell reacted with the copper.

But then, to their horror, the woman slowly got to her feet. "Is that the best you can do?" she snapped.

She walked over and greedily dived her hands into the fizzing box.

Instantly a ribbon of energy leapt across her body. Her human disguise melted away. She became a whirlwind of sparks. For a moment the room was a storm of raw power.

Then stillness.

The Cell rolled along the floor. Faraday picked it up. "Interesting," he muttered, handing it to Nadim.

The doorway appeared. Nadim, Wilma and Kipper knew what it was. They stepped into it. Suddenly Kipper saw the Viran man get up and move towards Tyler.

"Tyler!" Kipper yelled, leaping out of the doorway. "Look out!"

"Kipper!" yelled Wilma. "Come back!"

Kipper looked back. But the doorway had gone. Nadim and Wilma had vanished.

Now what?

Now the TimeWeb has power. The power of the Cell.

At first, the woman was friendly to Wilma and Nadim. Would you have trusted her?

Michael Faraday knew the Virans were after the Cell. Why did he get Tyler to hide it?

How did the Viran explode? What happened to her?

What will be the function of the Hub in the TimeWeb?

If the other missions – *The Jewel in the Hub* and *The Matrix Mission* – have been successful, then the TimeWeb has to work, if only to find Kipper ...

So now you must read:
The TimeWeb
... Every second is precious, so hurry!

History: downloaded!
Michael Faraday

In the story, we meet a young Michael Faraday while he was an apprentice bookbinder in London, in about 1805. At that time, books were not bound in covers but sold as loose printed pages. For extra money, a customer could have these pages bound together and covered.

As Michael stitched covers on to books he couldn't help reading the pages themselves, especially if they were about science.

Magnet

After finishing his apprenticeship, Michael became a scientist. He was the first to realize that it was possible to turn the force from a magnet into electricity. He also realized that the reverse is true – electricity can turn some metals, such as iron, into magnets.

Thanks to Faraday's discoveries many inventions followed, from the light switch to the long distance telegram. The age of electricity had begun.

For more information, see the Time Chronicles website:
www.oxfordprimary.co.uk/timechronicles

Glossary

bookbinder *(page 7)* A craftsman who ties printed pages together, and then covers them to make a book. *The light came from a bookbinder's shop, full of leather-covered books.*

cylinders *(page 14)* A cylinder looks like a tube with circular ends. Here a cylinder is a name for a type of glass jar that scientists use. *Above a large fireplace were shelves stacked with bottles and tubes, cylinders, coils of wire and copper sheets.*

dimly *(page 13)* With a faint light, not brightly. *A single lamp glowed dimly in the gloom.*

glanced *(page 14)* Looked at something quickly or briefly. *Nadim glanced nervously around.*

lodestone *(page 15)* A rock that naturally attracts iron. Another word for a magnet. *"It is a powerful magnet called a lodestone."*

magnet *(page 15)* A piece of metal that is able to attract (and repel) some metals and other magnets.

Thesaurus: Another word for ...

dimly *(page 13)* dingily, hazily, gloomily, murkily.

Have you read them all yet?

Level 11:

Level 12:

Time Runners

Tyler: His Story

A Jack and Three Queens

Mission Victory

The Enigma Plot

The Thief Who Stole Nothing

More great fiction from Oxford Children's:

www.winnie-the-witch.com

www.dinosaurcove.co.uk

About the Authors

Roderick Hunt MBE - creator of best-loved characters Biff, Chip, Kipper, Floppy and their friends. His first published stories were those he told his two sons at bedtime. Rod lives in Oxfordshire, in a house not unlike the house in the Magic Key adventures. In 2008, Roderick received an MBE for services to education, particularly literacy.

Roderick Hunt's son **David Hunt** was brought up on his father's stories and knows the world of Biff, Chip and Kipper intimately. His love of history and a good story has sparked many new ideas, resulting in the *Time Chronicles* series. David has had a successful career in the theatre, most recently working on scripts for Jude Law's *Hamlet* and *Henry V,* as well as Derek Jacobi's *Twelfth Night.*

Joint creator of the best-loved characters Biff, Chip, Kipper, Floppy and their friends, **Alex Brychta MBE** has brought each one to life with his fabulous illustrations, which are known and loved in many schools today. Following the Russian occupation of Czechoslovakia, Alex Brychta moved with his family from Prague to London. He studied graphic design and animation, before moving to the USA where he worked on animation for Sesame Street. Since then he has devoted many years of his career to *Oxford Reading Tree,* bringing detail, magic and humour to every story! In 2012 Alex received an MBE for services to children's literature.

Roderick Hunt and Alex Brychta won the prestigious Outstanding Achievement Award at the Education Resources Awards in 2009.

43

Levelling info for parents

What do the levels mean?

Read with Biff Chip & Kipper First Chapter Books have been designed by educational experts to help children develop as readers.

Each book is carefully levelled to allow children to make gradual progress and to feel confident and enjoy reading.

The Oxford Levels you will see on these books are used by teachers and are based on years of research in schools. Below is a summary of what each Oxford Level means, so that you can help your child to improve and enjoy their reading.

The books at Level 11 (Brown Book Band):

At this level, the sentence structures are becoming longer and more complex. The story plot may be more involved and there is a wider vocabulary. However, the proportion of unknown words used per paragraph/page is still carefully controlled to help build their reading stamina and allow children to read independently.

This level mostly covers characterisation through characters' actions and words rather than through description. The story may be organised in various ways, e.g. chronologically, thematically, sequentially, as relevant to the text type and subject.

The books at Level 12 (Grey Book Band):

At this level, the sentences are becoming more varied in structure and length. Though still straightforward, more inference may be required, e.g. in dialogue to work out who is speaking. Again, the story may be organised in various ways: chronologically, thematically, sequentially, etc., so that children can reflect on how the organisation helps the reader to understand the text.

The *Times Chronicles* books are also ideal for older children who feel less confident and need more practice in order to build stamina. The text is written to be age and ability appropriate, but also engaging, motivating and funny, making them a pleasure for children to read at this stage of their reading development.

OXFORD
UNIVERSITY PRESS

Great Clarendon Street, Oxford, OX2 6DP,
United Kingdom

Oxford University Press is a department of the University of Oxford.
It furthers the University's objective of excellence in research, scholarship,
and education by publishing worldwide. Oxford is a registered trade mark
of Oxford University Press in the UK and in certain other countries

Text © Roderick Hunt and David Hunt

Text written by David Hunt, based on the original characters
created by Roderick Hunt and Alex Brychta

Illustrations © Alex Brychta

The moral rights of the authors have been asserted

Database rights Oxford University Press (maker)

First published 2010
This edition published in 2015

British Library Cataloguing in Publication Data
Data available

978-0-19-273909-4

1 3 5 7 9 10 8 6 4 2

Paper used in the production of this book is a natural, recyclable product
made from wood grown in sustainable forests. The manufacturing process
conforms to the environmental regulations of the country of origin.

Printed in China

Acknowledgements: The publisher and authors would like to thank the following
for their permission to reproduce photographs and other copyright material:

P38tl TsR/Shutterstock; **P38ml** World History Archive/Alamy; **p38ml** Ecoasis/
Shutterstock; **p38bl** Sibrikov Valery/Shutterstock; **p38m** Valentin Agapov/
Shutterstock; **p38br** Bronwyn Photo/Shutterstock; **p38-39** Jakub Krechowicz/
Shutterstock; Blaz Kure/Shutterstock; **p39m** Mary Evans Picture Library;
p38br Paul Vinten/ Shutterstock

Book quiz answers
1 b
2 A Viran
3 The whole box fizzed with a massive charge of power.